The FAB Four

ORCHARD BOOKS
96 Leonard Street, London EC2A 4XD
Orchard Books Australia
32/45-51 Huntley Street, Alexandria, NSW 2015
ISBN 1 84121 362 4
First published in Great Britain in 2003
A paperback original

A CIP catalogue record for this book is available from the British Library.
1 3 5 7 9 10 8 6 4 2
Printed in Great Britain

All for One

Ros
Asquith

ORCHARD BOOKS

One

I never knew that I was lucky till now... thought Eclaire, as she slumped miserably on a beanbag the size of Everest, gazing sadly around her lovely big pink room. She looked at the gorgeous, big, fat, violet and purple satiny cushions, and the big fat soft bed with its plump, patchwork duvet. She wiggled her toes in the deep-pile carpet and buried her head in the arms of a teddy the size of a grizzly bear... She sighed deeply and looked dolefully out of the window at the garden with its swings, fish pond, big, fat guinea pigs and big, fat red roses cascading over the walls. It had never looked more beautiful to Eclaire.

She turned sadly to gaze in the mirror at herself, a once happy girl, as big and as round as everything else in the room. "I never realised just how lucky I am... and now it's too late." And Eclaire watched herself in the mirror, as first one, then two, then dozens of big fat tears rolled down her cheeks and dripped off her chin.

It had all started that morning. Mr and Mrs Pinn, Eclaire's annoyingly thin parents, who looked as slim and useful as two well-sharpened pencils, had knocked on her door and said, "Claire, we need a little talk."

Oh, no, Eclaire had thought. They're going to try to force me onto another one of their ghastly diets.

But, in fact, it was much worse, which was why Eclaire, usually a ray of sunshine, was sunk in such a deep gloom that she felt even the Fab Four couldn't help her...

And it seemed that something awful was happening next door, too.

"Oh, no! That's dreadful news. What *are* you going to do? What are *we* going to do?"

These were the first words that Lizzy heard as she broke yet another comb on her mad, tangled mane – not for nothing was she called Frizzy Lizzy – and slid down the bannister to breakfast.

"Urgh!" Her adorable brother Ernie had plastered the bannister in *Slimo.*

"But how on earth will we all cope? Lizzy will be *miserable...*" were the next words Lizzy heard, apart from the rude words she herself had just uttered on discovering that the *Slimo* had stuck fast to her jeans, which had stuck fast to the bannisters. Struggling to wrench herself free, Lizzy craned her neck towards the kitchen door. Her mum was on the phone.

"No. No, I won't say anything," Lizzy heard her mum whisper into the receiver, as she twisted herself free – ripping off her pocket in the process

– and burst into the kitchen.

"What's up?" asked Lizzy, as she poured a vast helping of *Krisped Riceys* – and screamed.

"Aaaaaargh! There's a Mighty Mammoth-Murderer in my cereal!"

"Ernie!" shouted Lizzy's mum. "If you put your Doom Warriors in the cereal packets *one more time...*"

But Lizzy's nerdy brother, Ernie, was already out of the door and skateboarding to school.

"When he gets back, I will get him and I will mince him into very little pieces and feed him to the cat. He's wrecked my jeans!" Lizzy turned to her mum. "So what's the matter?" she asked.

"Nothing," said Mrs Wigan. "Whatever makes you think that something is up?"

"I just heard you saying that everything was dreadful!"

"Oh, oh... that was, um, another Karate Gang robbery. They've ransacked two of the stores on the other side of town," said Mrs Wigan unconvincingly. "Honestly, it's getting like Chicago round here."

"But, you said that I'd be miserable!" insisted

Lizzy. "Why would the Karate Gang make *me* miserable?"

"Oh, no. Th-that was another Lizzy. You know, um, Lizzy from work. She lives near there and she's worried that they might mug her..." said her mum, reddening.

Lizzy knew it was true that the Karate Gang had been doing scary things in the neighbourhood for about three months. She also knew that they always seemed to attack stores and offices at night, not people. They ransacked places that were then sold off cheaply, because people were too scared to re-open their shops. No one, not even PC Bigfoot, had got to the bottom of it yet. The gang dressed in white suits and red bandanas and wore masks... but they hadn't mugged anyone – yet. And, anyway, Lizzy was sure that there wasn't another Lizzy in her mum's life. She'd have noticed. What was her mum trying to hide?

That evening, her parents mooched around with faces like wet Wednesdays and whispered in corners like parents do when they know something horrible has happened and are trying to hide it. But they wouldn't tell Lizzy or Ernie what was up, so Lizzy knew that there was only one thing for it. Phone the Fab Four!

And so it was that at 6:00 that evening, Owl and Flash bundled up Lizzy's stairs and demanded to know what was up.

"Something horrible is happening to my family," said Lizzy. "My folks are pretending they're worried about the Karate gang. But I *know* it isn't that. I don't know what's wrong," she went on miserably. "I just know *something* is. And I want *us* to find out."

"Well, it *might* be the Karate Gang," said Flash. "My mum's worried about them... Anyway, we can't start without Eclaire," she said, reasonably enough.

"It's n-not like her to be late. Maybe she g-got held up in b-bad traffic?" said Owl with a grin.

"Ha ha," said Lizzy, pulling a face. Eclaire only lived next door. Lizzy banged hard on the wall between their bedrooms. No reply. She banged again, much harder. There was a feeble knocking back.

"Oh, well. If she won't come here, let's go there,"

said Lizzy crossly.

But it wasn't that simple. When Owl, Flash and Lizzy knocked on Eclaire's front door, her mum answered it.

"I'm afraid Claire's not very well," said Mrs Pinn, barring their way.

"Oh, please, Mrs Pinn. We'll cheer her up," pleaded Lizzy.

"Yes," sighed Mrs Pinn, forcing a smile and looking more than ever like a pencil that has been sharpened to breaking point. "Perhaps you will..."

At last, she let them in.

But, when they got upstairs, the fourth member of the Fab Four was hunched miserably in her beanbag, a tear hovering on her chin...

"Eclairykins! What on Earth is the matter?" shouted Lizzy, surprised to see her ever-jolly pal so gloomy. "Are they putting you on another disgusting diet?"

But Eclaire just shook her head.

"Look, Eclaire. Lizzy's got a big problem, so why don't you try to help her? It might take your mind off your own stuff?" said the practical Flash, who was actually dying to tell some news of her own.

And so, with heavy hearts, the Fab Four made a circle and chanted:

"All for one and one for all
Fatty, skinny, short and tall
Frizzy, Flash, Owl and Eclaire
Stick together, foul or fair.

"Four for one and one for four
Funny, clever, rich and poor
Frizzy, Flash, Eclaire and Owl
Stick together, fair or foul."

"So, look," began Lizzy. "My folks are going round with faces like sad sardines and keep saying that something 'dreadful' is happening. Do any of you know what it might be?"

There was a long silence, during which everyone thought something different.

Obviously, Lizzy's parents are splitting up, thought Flash, who remembered the day her dad left home, as though it were yesterday. Sometimes, though, she wondered whether she could actually remember what he *looked* like, or whether it was just the photo her mum kept beside her bed.

Owl was thinking, with her usual taste for melodrama, Oh, no. Someone's ill. One of her folks is dying and they don't dare tell Lizzy and Ernie. Oh, horrors!

But, of course, neither Flash nor Owl liked to say what was going through their minds, so they both twiddled their fingers and sighed sympathetically, as if racking their brains.

It was Eclaire who eventually broke the silence. "I think my mum has been talking to your mum," she said.

"Yes?" said Lizzy.

"And she's probably told her our bad news..." sniffed Eclaire, furiously blowing her nose.

"W-what bad news?" asked Lizzy, fearing the worst.

Flash and Owl immediately changed their dramatic scenarios. Now, it was not Lizzy's folks, but the Pinns who were splitting up or dying.

"My dad's lost his job," said Eclaire flatly.

Everyone sighed with relief, or was it disappointment?

"Is that all?" said Lizzy.

"Well, that's not the end of the world," said Flash. "He's a manager, for goodness sake. And a local councillor. Everyone knows your dad. He'll just get another job."

"He has," mumbled Eclaire. "He's been offered another one."

"Well, that's all right then. What's all the fuss

about?" said Lizzy, annoyed that all the attention was moving away from her. "That can't be the reason *my* folks are miserable, can it?"

"Oh. No. Maybe your folks don't mind that we're going to move house," said Eclaire. "Maybe they don't care that their favourite neighbours, who've lived next door all these years, are moving to the other side of the country in just three months' time! But I *do* care! And... and I won't even have my brothers with me!" Eclaire's annoyingly thin and handsome older brothers were starting university soon. And this was the first time she had realised how much she was going to miss them, even though they *were* so thin and handsome.

"You're going to move house?" chorused Owl, Flash and Lizzy. "But *where*?"

"Down south," said Eclaire flatly. "That's where Dad's got another job! And it's a much worse job! So we'll have to move to a horrid little pokey grotty flat, smaller than..."

"Smaller than mine?" said Flash quietly. *She* lived in a tower block, in a flat the size of a button. And it was just her and her mum and a lodger, so she had to sleep on a camp bed in the titchy living-room. *She* didn't complain.

But Eclaire rattled on regardless. "And my room will be smaller than..."

"M-mine?" asked Owl, thinking of her own room, which was barely bigger than an ant's matchbox, or would be, if ants used matches.

"And the school is really rough..." continued Eclaire, not listening.

"Like the one I'm g-going to next year?" asked Owl.

"Oh, I'm sorry," said Eclaire, "I know I sound like a spoilt brat. But I'm going to miss my lovely, big, fat house and room and bed and everything. Most of all," she gulped, "I'm going to miss all of you! I can't imagine life without the Fab Four."

"And *we* can't imagine life without *you*," said Lizzy, flinging her arms around her big, cuddly friend.

And, of course, the others felt just the same. In fact, now the news had sunk in, they all felt almost as desperate as Eclaire. Lovely, bouncy Eclaire, who made the most magnificent sweets and wrote the most magnificent poems and was destined to be the world's first poetic chef, had always been there to cheer them up when they were down. Suddenly, she seemed to be the most vital member of the Fab Four.

Lizzy gazed at her best pal, who had lived next door all her life. As she did so, a host of magic moments paraded through her imagination. Lizzy remembered their first day at playgroup, when she and Eclaire had both clung together and refused to speak to anyone else, until a horrid little girl covered in ribbons had poked them and lisped, "Are you Thiamethe twinth?" She also remembered their second day, when they had both firmly announced to their mothers, "We aren't going! We've already been! We went *yesterday*!" And she remembered how, when they got older and braver, they used to wee in the dolly's tea set and offer it to the teacher as lemonade. Eclaire had seen Lizzy through all this – and much, much more. She must be saved at all costs.

"Eclaire, we can't let it happen! We just can't!"

"Never!" said Flash.

"If one g-goes, all go!" added Owl.

"Yeah!" said Lizzy. "That's what we'll do. We'll get our folks to move as well! Easy!"

"You are all bonkers," said Flash. "Our folks all have jobs! At least, I hope so..." Flash lived in constant fear that her own mum would lose her part-time job as a school dinner lady.

"Oh, they'll find jobs," said Lizzy, thinking that there must be schools and chemists and dentists everywhere needing marvellous handy people like their parents.

"Er, I don't think so," whispered Owl shyly. "Loretta's not g-going to like it, for one."

Lizzy frowned. She had forgotten about Owl's glamorous big sister, who had just started drama school, and was unlikely to want to move. In fact, her own brother, Ernie, wasn't going to like it either. Then, she suddenly brightened, feeling the kind of surging excitement in her head that made her understand the expression "brain wave" for the very first time.

"Wait! I know! I know!" shouted Lizzy. "It's so simple! Why didn't I think of it before?"

"What?" said Eclaire eagerly. The loving attention of her friends had cheered her up, but now she felt that they were grasping at straws. And she still hadn't mentioned her biggest worry...

But Lizzy suddenly looked really confident. She paused triumphantly, as three pairs of eyes swivelled towards her. "Eclaire can move in with us!" she said, to Eclaire. "My folks think of you as a second daughter already! And your folks will be pleased, you know, one less mouth to feed..."

Luckily, Eclaire was laughing. "Well, I'm like about *three* mouths to feed, I know that. But, Lizzy, I think my parents are a bit fond of me. I'm, well, a bit fond of them, too..."

"Oh. Yeah. I suppose you are, in a way," admitted Lizzy, blushing. She felt hurt that Eclaire was rejecting her offer.

"But I'd love to, of course, if you think they'd say yes," said Eclaire quickly. And, at that moment, she really did believe that it would be much, much better to stay with her friend than to move to somewhere where she knew no one at all...

"Well that's what we'll do, then," said Lizzy. "I declare that we shall all:

a) Try to persuade our parents to move south with Eclaire

b) If that fails, get Eclaire's parents to let her stay with me! We will report back tomorrow evening at 6:30 at my place. All those in favour, say 'Meringue'." And everyone did.

Lizzy raced next door.

"Why didn't you tell me they were moving?" she asked angrily.

"I was going to, of course, but Mrs Pinn begged me not to. She's embarrassed about Percy. He's always been so successful and she feels ashamed. She wanted to see first if he could find another job..."

"But, poor Eclaire!"

"Well, poor all of them. Mrs Pinn says that Claire's taking it very badly. She's worried that she isn't eating!"

"But she's been trying to get her to go on a diet for years!" said Lizzy, amazed.

"I know. Oh, it's so sad."

"You'll miss them, won't you, Mum?"

"Oh, yes. I mean Percy's a bit pompous, but he's awfully good-hearted, and does so much for the neighbourhood. And Elaine is, you know, an awful snob, but very kind in a crisis. They've been our neighbours ever since we moved here, when I was expecting you, and Elaine was expecting Claire...the only time I can remember Mrs Pinn being far from thin!"

Lizzy knew that she had got her mum into just the right kind of sentimental mood. She had softened her up – now was the time to strike.

"Eclaire must seem like a second daughter to you, Mum," she said, in a wheedling tone, sidling up and slipping an arm round her mum's shoulders.

"Yes," said her mum. "And almost like a sister to you. Poor Lizzy."

"So I've got a brilliant idea! Why don't we all move too?"

"Lizzy! Don't be ridiculous! What about Ernie? What about *my* job? What about Dad's job? Jobs don't just grow on trees, you know!"

"But you'll be saving a young girl's sanity! Two young girls' sanities," said Lizzy articulately.

"Don't be so melodramatic. You can see Claire in the holidays!"

Lizzy felt she was losing the advantage, which was true.

"Well, then. I've an even better idea that means you won't have to do anything!"

"And what's that?" asked Lizzy's mum, with a rather beady look.

"Let's ask Eclaire to live with us!"

There was a silence.

Then Lizzy's mum said in her very kindest voice, "You know it won't work, Lizzy. The Pinns want

Claire to live with them. She's their daughter. They *love* her. And we don't have the room."

"She can sleep in my room!"

"Lizzy! That's enough."

"I can't live without Eclaire! She can't live without me!" stormed Lizzy and charged upstairs, fuming at the hopeless meanness of the adult world. It would be perfectly simple for her parents to let Eclaire live in their house. And how was she going to break the news to Eclaire that her best friend's parents were rejecting her? WHY was everything so *unfair*?

Two

Owl arrived at Lizzy's at 6:32 the next day, only to find all the others already sitting in a gloomy circle. They had cleared a space in Lizzy's chaotic bedroom, but were still surrounded by her brush and comb collections and hair potions. In other circumstances, seeing Eclaire and Flash and Lizzy surrounded by a mad collection of conditioners, daft-looking serums and anti-frizz products would have made Owl laugh, but one look at their faces told her that things had not gone according to plan. But, she had suspected that this would be the case, and had spent all night dreaming up a plan. Now, she was bursting to tell it. But she waited patiently while everyone told their stories.

Flash's mum had laughed 'like a hyena' at the thought of moving. The chance of finding another cheap flat was slim enough, let alone one within a bus ride of a decent job. She had scrimped and saved enough, thank you very much, and she didn't think that it was the end of the world for Claire to have to move. Loads of kids did it, and Claire should be thankful that she had two parents and a father with a job!

Flash didn't repeat quite all of this, for fear of hurting Eclaire's feelings, but she said enough to make it clear how her mother had felt. As she finished her story, Flash shrugged her shoulders, hoping that the others would notice her brand new bra. She had been dying to tell the Fab Four about it, but they were all too bothered burbling on about Eclaire. It worked!

"Flash! You've got a bra!" said Lizzy, gratifyingly.

"Oh, it's *so* unfair," said Eclaire, who seemed, thought Flash, to have turned overnight from the life and soul of the party into a total whingebucket. "I'm big everywhere except in the chest department. It's so typical that slim, sporty old Flash should be the first one to need a bra!"

The others felt it was unfair too. Owl thought it rather bad timing, considering Eclaire was supposed to be the centre of attention. She gazed enviously at Flash, thinking she was about as much in need of a bra as, well, a prawn was in need of a haircut.

Lizzy, inwardly fuming, gave Flash a big pat on the back.

"Well done, Flash! First past the post as usual!"

"Yeah, th-that's great," said Owl. "I expect I'll be getting a bra in about t-ten years' time. And maybe I'll find a couple of things to put in it a few years after th-that..."

"Oh, Owly, it'll happen soon enough," said Flash, going rather red. She had expected lots of excitement and it seemed that everyone was jealous instead. Maybe the Fab Four were not what they used to be...

"It's *so* unfair. No wonder kids run away from home," said Eclaire.

"I think kids who run away from home probably have better reasons than because they don't need a bra!" said Flash grimly.

"I don't mean that," snapped Eclaire. "We've talked enough about your stupid bra! I meant that my folks wouldn't let me go and live with Lizzy!"

"Oh, no!" said Lizzy. "I don't believe it! And my folks would have *loved* to have you," she lied.

"Would they?" Would they really?" asked Eclaire. "Maybe your mum could persuade my mum..."

"Mmmmmmmmmm," said Lizzy, pretending to blow her nose.

"We've hardly talked at *all* about my bra as it happens. Or about how it happens to be quite a *big* size! The lady at the shop told my mum that I had a lovely figure!" Flash scowled. "Anyway, Owl, what did *your* folks say? Maybe *you* can be the one who moves south with Eclaire? Then, we can have two lots of the Tremendous Two and be the Fab Four once in a blue moon... Or maybe you can all be the Terrific Trio and I'll be the 'Orrible One! Which might be a *lot* better than it is now!" And, with that, Flash jumped up and made for the door.

But, getting out of Lizzy's room was not as easy as it looked. Flash collided with a pyramid of hair potions, skidded on a bottle of volumising mousse and somersaulted into a nest of hairbrushes. It was not the dignified exit she had intended. When she stood up and caught sight of herself in the mirror, covered in sticky foaming mousse, to which at least four combs, a couple of brushes that looked remarkably like hedgehogs, and about fifty hairpins were glued, she didn't know whether to laugh or cry. Luckily, she chose the former.

Eclaire saved the day by reverting to her usual kind character. She gave Flash a bear hug, generously covering herself in foam as well.

"Honestly, Lizzy, I thought you'd stopped worrying about your hair being frizz... I mean, curly," giggled Eclaire.

"You two!" said Lizzy, whipping out her camera. "You look like porcupines in a snowdrift. Now come on, Owly. What *did* your mum say?"

"M-my mother laughed too," said Owl. "B-but my sister Loretta went completely nuts. She said that I was a selfish little p-pig trying to ruin her great career as a star!"

"That's so mean," said Lizzy. "You were only trying to help a friend."

"I know. B-but I have a b-better idea," said Owl in her tiny voice, thankful that at last she could reveal her big idea. "I got a leaflet yesterday about the school fair. They raised a f-fortune. So, why don't we have a street fair and raise enough money to pay Mr Pinn, say, six months' salary? Then he'll have loads of t-time to look for a new job round here!"

Not for the first time, the rest of the Fab Four turned to their smallest member in amazement.

"Yes! Brilliant!" exclaimed Lizzy and Flash.

"We can't possibly!" said Eclaire. "You don't know how much my dad earns! It'll be far more than we can raise!"

"Well, then, two months. Two months is a long time!"

"Yes, but even that..."

"How much does he earn?" asked Flash.

Eclaire went very quiet.

"I *think*," she said, "I *think* it's about £20,000 a year."

Everyone went very very quiet.

"T-two months would be £3,333, then," said Owl.

The others looked at her, as they always did, in awe. It was amazing that such a small, shy person had such a very large brain.

"You'll come in really handy when it's time for GCSEs, Owly," said Flash. "We could take turns to borrow you and put you in our pockets. Much more reliable than a calculator and no batteries needed. Of course, you'll have to stay small – no bras till you're 17, OK?"

Owl smiled weakly.

"Look, if a little primary school can raise £2,100 in one afternoon's summer fair, then we can have a big event with all the kids in the neighbourhood. We can rope in little Brian Hayseed and Loretta and Ernie as special helpers and we can make it go on till midnight and we're bound to raise more!" Flash was really enthusiastic now. "We'll all go off and get as many ideas as possible and meet tomorrow at my place – with plans."

"But, wait," said Owl, who had, in the middle of the night, got so excited at her idea that she had not noticed one enormous loophole. She was amazed that Flash hadn't spotted it either. "Th-there's a bit of a hitch..."

"What?" said Flash, impatient as ever to be off and doing something.

"W-e-ll. We're n-not a school or a charity or anything. I mean, people won't come and give us money, just like that."

"They will if it's a fair. You don't ask where the money's going to if you go to a fair. It just goes to the people who run the fairground," said Flash.

"Y-yes, but this isn't a fair, is it?" said Owl. "Not unless you know a handy rollercoaster operator who'll lend us the stuff. This will be, er, apple bobbing and cake stalls and stuff that *we* can do..."

"We'll say it's for a good cause," said Flash determinedly. "Which it is!"

"Yeah..." said Lizzy, feeling a twinge of doubt. "We can say it's for a needy girl, who is in danger of having her life ruined for ever..."

"Because she hasn't got a bra!" finished Eclaire.

"Yeah! Let's call it BRA. People will be too embarrassed to ask what that is, but if they do, we can say, um, Building Real Action, or some twaddle like that. Loads of charities have names like that," said Flash.

"No, seriously, can't we think up a name that is, like, well, not exactly a lie..." muttered Lizzy. "How about *Child in Need*? Or *Save the Child*?"

"No," said Owl, worried that her idea was disappearing fast. "They're too like the names of other charities. We'll get s-sued."

"I know." said Flash "*Children's Rights*. After all, it is our right not to move house just because some old fogies make us!"

"Yeah, yeah. Hang on a minute," said Lizzy, her eyes shining. "What was your mum's maiden name, you know, before she married?"

"Bishop," said Eclaire. "What's that got to do with it?"

"I *thought* so! That's it! We'll call it *The Bishop's Needy Children Fund!* It may not be completely honest, but it's not a lie either..."

"Lizzy, you are a genius," said Flash. "Now, just how are we going to organise it all?"

"Um, I've th-thought of another hitch," mumbled Owl. "Where c-can we have it? I mean, none of us have, um, gardens big enough... not even you, Eclaire."

"In the street, of course! *Our* street," said Eclaire. "It's good for stuff like that because it's a dead end. We had a brilliant Jubilee party here, didn't we, Lizzy?"

"Er..." said Lizzy, who had wanted to watch the Jubilee fireworks and parades and, instead, had been really bored pouring orange juice for a horde of sticky toddlers. "It was OK, I suppose... But this one will be *miles* better – we aren't just going to have a few trestle tables and old biscuits. Maybe we could get some stars to come. How about Sharon Skinner and Danny Valentine?"

"Get real, Lizzy," sneered Flash. "I can just imagine them saying, 'Oh, look, an invitation to present the raffle prizes at *The Bishop's Fund* street fair. That's one we can't miss! That'll be the highlight of our year.'"

"Yes, but maybe we can get someone local and famous! You know, we could ask someone like that woman who does the weather on TV. She lives just round the corner. Or, we could try writing to a few really famous people and see if they turn up..."

Lizzy trailed off. She was beginning to think that what they really needed was a fairy godmother to fly past, scattering a few billion golden dubloons...

"I think that's a great idea, Lizzy," said Eclaire, who had now completely cheered up. "I'll take charge of that, although you can help Owly, seeing as you are so literary. You could write to actors, and I could write to celebrity chefs."

"OK," said Lizzy. "As chair of this urgent meeting, I declare that the Fab Four's mission is to raise £3,333 in exactly one month, to save the Pinns! Owly, you can organise street theatre. Get loads of performers and mime artists and jugglers and stuff like that."

"Oh. Sure. Easy," said Owl, quaking at the thought. It was all very well being interested in theatre, but where was she going to find a whole gang of performers?

Lizzy surged on. "Eclaire, what would you like to do? Food, obviously. You can make a few thousand batches of Nuclear

Nougat and Karamel Kalashnikovs. Flash, you can be in charge of sports and games. Races, apple bobbing, hook the duck, you know!"

"And pony rides!" said Flash, the bit between her teeth.

"And we've all got to think of loads of stalls – bring-and-buy, jumble, books, records. We can turn out our houses and sell all our old stuff."

"Yes. But what are *you* going to do?" asked Flash, hitching up her bra strap rather obviously.

"I'll organise a mega raffle. We could raffle your bra, as you haven't got enough to fill such a big size yet, obviously!"

This unwise remark led to a rather vigorous pillow fight, which ended with all four girls rolling in hair potion and feathers.

"What on Earth is going on!" Lizzy's mum was standing at the door, aghast. "Oh, Harriet, you've got a bra! How exciting!" she said, giving Flash a hug.

"Um. Just rehearsing for one of Owl's theatre things," mumbled Lizzy crossly, through a mouthful of feathers.

"Well, you can rehearse cleaning this lot up

right now!" said her mum. "When you've rehearsed that, you can do the show for real, but I want this room spotless by 7:30!"

So, the second meeting of the Fab Four that week ended on a slightly more cheerful note than the first. And when they had finished tidying up, Lizzy's room was unrecognisable.

"Hey, Lizzy. You should keep it like this. You can see the floor!" said Eclaire, which was a cue for another pillow fight, except that, luckily, it was supper time.

Lizzy declared the meeting over, but just as the others were leaving, Eclaire turned to the others with a deadly serious expression on her face and said that she had something very, very important to say.

Oh no, what's up with her now, thought Flash, irritably.

"I just want to say one thing," said Eclaire with a huge smile. "THANK YOU, for doing this for me, my bestest friends."

Hmph, thought Flash. Maybe the Fab Four are OK, after all.

But, in her heart of hearts, Eclaire was feeling even more miserable than ever. What she hadn't felt able to say, even to her closest pals, was that her father was a changed man.

Lizzy guessed that all was not well in the Pinn house, and rang her later that night.

"I can't really talk for long," hissed Eclaire. "But you're right...you see...my dad's gone peculiar. He doesn't *do* anything any more. He just sits in his chair, staring into space... Oh, Lizzy, it's *terrible*."

Oh, thought Lizzy. Mr Pinn had always been such an energetic person, always raising money for good causes, sitting on committees, going off to important meetings, and complaining to the local paper about this and that. Lizzy had always thought that if he *had* been a pencil, he wouldn't be the kind of pencil that lies about broken with a chewed rubber, he would be the kind that is first out of the pencil case every morning, scribbling away feverishly all day. He was, in fact, maddeningly busy, according to Lizzy's mum...

"Don't worry," said Lizzy. "The Fab Four will fix it, you'll see."

Three

The following week was a mass of activity. Flash and Owl designed leaflets, which they photocopied at their schools.

It was Owl who insisted that the last line should be as small as possible. A little voice in her head, which she knew was her conscience, although she was trying very hard to ignore it, told her that as little attention as possible should be drawn to their 'white lie'.

Unfortunately, it wasn't until they'd done one hundred photocopies each that Flash noticed they'd missed the 't' out of 'mystery'. "Oh, well. We can pretend they're miserable celebrities if anyone asks," she thought.

"We all ought to wear fancy dress, I suppose," said Eclaire. "Then we might win. If we do, that would add to the dosh we make."

"Yeah, especially if one of us is the judge," grinned Flash, who really fancied togging herself up as Buffalo Bill.

Eclaire spent the whole week baking cakes and making vast batches of Chocwhizzers, Karamel Kalashnikovs, Nuclear Nougat, Fudgemallows, and Hot Chilli Fudge. But, she was feeling more miserable than ever. Her dad had hardly spoken for a week and her mother, who was a bag of nerves at the best of times, was so worried that she'd become even thinner than usual.

Still, Eclaire soldiered on. She and Owl wrote

letters to as many famous people as they could think of – including Prince Harry:

Dear H.R.H. Prince Harry,
You and your brother William are invited to attend our GRAND STREET FAIR on 20th June there will be lots of FUN and three million girls to choose from.
We will ~~be~~ give you masses of sweets. All you have to do is stand around a bit looking gorgeous. You can MAKE a speech if you like.

R.S.V.P. To OWL and Eclaire.

"I don't think we s-should exaggerate the numbers. I mean, he is a bit shy, isn't he? Perhaps if we just said *some* girls?" wondered Owl, who certainly knew a lot about shyness, even if she didn't have the faintest idea of how to write to a prince.

"No," said Eclaire. "Go for it."

The Fab Four combed the neighbourhood, rounding up support and begging and borrowing raffle prizes.

As they visited the shops on the high street, Eclaire suddenly turned to Lizzy. "Have you asked your mum to talk to mine about me moving in with you yet?" she asked anxiously.

"Not yet," said Lizzy, playing for time. "I thought it was better to wait till, er, she's finished this training thing at the chemist's, um..."

"Because, you know, I didn't like to say this to Owlee, but I don't really think this thing will work. Dad'll be pleased to have the money, but it's not like having a proper job...and they've already gone to look at flats and stuff... So I may *have* to move in with you..."

"Oh, I'm sure the fair *will* work," said Lizzy, blushing. "Anyway, Mum'll talk to your mum as soon as the fair's over." She glanced at Eclaire, who looked crestfallen. She didn't know how she was ever going to tell her best friend that Mrs Wigan had said 'no'. Maybe she and Eclaire would just have to run away together...

Most of the shops gave a bottle of wine or some biscuits or chocolates. The mobile phone shop even offered a brand new phone with a colour screen.

"I think there's a catch here," said Eclaire, reading the product information that the shop had given them. You have to pay line rental for the next zillion years with this 'free' handset."

"Hey, what a cheek! You can get them for half that price," said Lizzy. "Let's give that one back."

The greengrocer offered a sack of Brussels sprouts, which they politely turned down, but he said that he'd be happy to turn up and teach little children how to make edible necklaces instead.

"Brilliant!" said Lizzy. "We can have an edible necklace competition!"

Their biggest success was the fire service. They agreed to bring along a fire engine and park it at the end of the street, so that children could climb about on it and try on firemen's hats. "Good for business," winked Bert Drench, the officer in charge. "We'll get some of those kids coming back to join up soon enough. Anyway, it's all in a good cause, innit?'

"Yes, yes," blushed Flash.

"Have you noticed that the posher the shop, the meaner the promise?" asked Eclaire thoughtfully. "Mr Vine at the big wine merchants offered one measly bottle of plonk, whereas Mr Patel at the late-night shop offered a whole case of really nice-looking wine!"

"Yeah, and Mr Fleecem, the estate agent, wouldn't didn't give anything at all! He could easily have offered us a cottage," giggled Lizzy. "I mean, a cottage for them would be like a sack of sprouts for the greengrocer. They must be *rolling* in dosh."

"And the old folks' home gave us a bigger box of chocs than the one the solicitor gave us. And the solicitor has a Rolls Royce," said Eclaire, "just for sending people to jail, or whatever it is he does."

"But there was an exception," said Lizzy thoughtfully. "You know that guy who used to work in the garage?"

"Yes, Mr Chang. He used to give us extra sweets," said Eclaire.

"Exactly!" said Lizzy. "He was always nice. Well, now he owns that big new art store! And I went in there while you were at the fire station. And he said that they'd give us a whole year's supply of drawing materials for a primary school!"

Eclaire went very quiet.

"You mean he runs *Artsmart*?" she said quietly.

"Yeah," said Lizzy.

"So it's *him*. It's Mr Chang! And I used to think that he was nice..." said Eclaire, kicking the pavement.

"What's wrong?" asked Owl, wondering what had got into Eclaire.

"He's the bloke who put my dad out of a job. His company's the reason my dad has to move south."

"But why?" said Lizzy.

"Well, they're a better company, I suppose, than my dad's... That's why my dad's company has had to close down," said Eclaire, sadly.

"Oh. Sorry," said Lizzy, blushing. "Let's not take his offer, then."

"Yeah. I couldn't take it. It would just be so embarrassing..." Eclaire looked down at her feet.

So Lizzy went back and said that she was very sorry, but they couldn't take the drawing materials.

"But my son's school would love to have all that," said Mr Chang in astonishment. "Any school would."

"Perhaps you could just give it to your son's school, then," said Lizzy, her cheeks turning redder by the second. "I'm so sorry, b-but we... it...it's too hard to explain. Sorry. Bye." Mr Chang watched her go and scratched his head in puzzlement.

That evening, the Fab Four all met up at Owl's place. Owl chaired the meeting. It was extremely difficult, at the best of times, to meet comfortably in Owl's room, but as everyone had bought pens, paper, leaflets and lists, it seemed even more crowded than usual. But, Owl was pleased to notice that everyone was in a good mood. "R-right. First let's look at the r-raffle. How's it going, Lizzy?"

Lizzy proudly waved the list of promises.

RAFFLE PRIZES

Case of Wine.
Bottle of Whiskey
3 barrels of ginger beer
1 Bottle 'measly plonk'
6 bottles of Lemonade
4 boxes of choccies
18 Boxes of Biccies
One choccy cake.
Dinner for 2 any Monday night at the 'GREECY SPUNE'
2 Cinema seats any Wednesday matinee
A Free dog shampoo and pedicure at Paula's Pet Parlour
2 SunBed sessions at Cinders' Tanning Salon
Cut + BlowDry at Sweeney's Barber
Painting by Local Artist, MAMATISSE
An Electric Kettle
A mop + Duster set

EXTRAS:
Fire Engine
Ice cream stall
Edible necklace competition

"Excellent!" said Owl. "And, um, f-food going OK?"

Eclaire reeled off a list of everything that she had made already. It sounded like enough to feed an army.

Flash had done even better. She had roped in

the boy scouts, the people from woodcraft evening class, the girl guides, the old folks' home and about half a dozen other assorted groups to run stalls and games. She had also got Astra Turf, the horoscope writer from the local paper, to come and do fortune telling. But, her best stroke had been persuading the stables that she worked for to come and give pony rides.

Owl, meanwhile, had organised the Incredible Kids' Cabaret. She had persuaded the local poet, Orpheus Clang, who regularly had his verses printed in the local paper, to give a reading.

This was the Cabaret Programme:

"Tiger Boy!" said Flash, Lizzy and Eclaire at once.

"Oh, he's amazing," said Owl, surprised that they hadn't picked out the performing fleas, or...but she preferred not to think of the other thing... "He turns into a tiger in front of your very eyes!" she enthused, hoping to keep everyone's mind on Tiger Boy.

"Really? You've seen it?"

"Erm, no. But loads of other people have." Then Owl whispered, "Rumour has it that his m-mother has leopard blood..."

There was an awed silence after this, until Eclaire squinted very hard at the Cabaret leaflet.

"Owly," she said. "What's this?"

Owl froze. "W-what?" she asked innocently.

"THIS," said Eclaire, pointing to the very tiny words at the very bottom of the leaflet.

"Erm, well, they h-haven't actually said they *won't* come..." muttered Owl.

"*Owl!* You can't say that the royals are coming!

We'll be sued!"

"I've thought of that," whispered Owl. "We can have little Harry Hawkins and William Snagg dressed up as p-princes in case."

"Oh, well, in for a penny, in for a pound, I suppose," laughed Eclaire...

Four

"Isn't it wonderful to see Eclaire bouncing back with a sparkle in her eye?" said Mrs Pinn to Mr Pinn late that evening.

"Hmmmmmmmm," said Mr Pinn, gazing into space.

Mrs Pinn had recently been getting extremely worried about her daughter. The sight of Eclaire off her food had sent her spiralling into a frenzy. Considering that she spent half her life trying to get her daughter to eat less, even Mrs Pinn could see that this was ironic. But, since Eclaire had been organising the fair, Mrs Pinn had begun to cheer up a fraction. Now, she was hoping that she might get her husband to cheer up, too.

"It's just marvellous all the girls being involved in raising money for charity, isn't it?" she continued in a bright, brittle voice that went through Mr Pinn's head like a road drill.

"Hmmmmm," said Mr Pinn.

"Any news on the job front?" squeaked Mrs Pinn nervously. She was still hoping that Mr Pinn's company would find him another job in this area. He had been told that there was a slim chance.

"Hmmmmmmmmm," said Mr Pinn.

"Oh, good! What?" asked Mrs Pinn, grinning from ear to ear.

"Hmmmmmmm," said Mr Pinn, falling fast asleep in his chair, as he so often did nowadays.

"Oh, dear." Mrs Pinn put her head in her hands. Sometimes, she felt that life was like a see-saw. As one thing went right, another went wrong straight away, so you felt like a leaf tossed about in a storm. A tear ran down her cheek.

"What's up, Mum?' said Eclaire, who couldn't sleep for the excitement of the fair, which was in just two days time. She had come downstairs for a glass of water.

"Oh, nothing," trilled Mrs Pinn. "Nothing at all."

"So why are you crying?"

"Onions," lied Mrs Pinn, grabbing the kitchen knife and a garlic clove. She looked, Eclaire was alarmed to notice, thinner and more fraught than ever.

"Mum, that is not onion, it is garlic. Look, don't worry about Dad. He'll be OK. We'll *all* be OK. The Fab Four will see to that."

"And pigs will fly," sighed Mrs Pinn. "You're not superheroes, you know – and neither is your father."

Eclaire gazed sadly at her snoring dad. He had *always* been a superhero to Eclaire, she realised. He had been a dad who was always working hard and bossing people around and being a councillor and writing letters to local papers about the litter in the streets and being generally in charge. Now he was looking, for the first time, well...old.

Eclaire felt a wave of love for her dad that she hadn't felt before. She had always felt proud of him and sometimes slightly scared of him. Now she wanted to give him a huge hug.

"It'll be OK," she said to her mum. "Trust me."

The next day, Eclaire got a shock.

"Isn't it marvellous," announced Mrs Apex, her head teacher, at assembly. "Li's father has given us a whole year's supply of drawing materials. I would like you all to write letters to Mr Wei Chang to thank him."

"Oh, no," thought Lizzy. "It's Li's dad who put Eclaire's dad out of a job!" She gazed along the row at Li, a quiet boy who had only joined the school that term. He was blushing at having his dad's name mentioned in assembly. Then Lizzy stole a look at Eclaire, who was bright red too, but with fury.

At break, despite Lizzy and Flash's attempts to stop her, Eclaire marched up to Li and told him exactly what she thought.

"My dad's firm has gone bust because of your dad!" she spluttered. "And my dad's been working in this town for years and he's been a councillor and *everything*. And *your* dad's only just moved here!"

Li looked at the ground and scuffed his trainers. The sight of his blue and silver trainers, which were the most expensive brand, made Eclaire feel like exploding.

"Don't you come anywhere near me!" she shouted. "And tell your dad that we don't need his stupid art stuff to save my dad! We can do it without him! The fair on Saturday *will* save my dad, and if I see you anywhere *near* it, then you will be mincemeat!" Then, to Lizzy's complete astonishment, Eclaire punched Li hard in the stomach.

"Ouch!" cried Eclaire, reeling back. "He's made of iron!"

"How dare you, Claire!" Mrs Apex swooped out of nowhere and inserted herself between them. "We do *not* have violence at this school. Apologise to Li at once." But Eclaire was too upset and angry to apologise.

Later that day Eclaire found a note in her school bag.

"Don't try that again. I'm a black belt. And so are my friends."

"Oh, no," said Eclaire to Lizzy, as they walked home. "Is that judo or karate? Do you think they'll lie in wait for us?"

"Course not," said Lizzy, sounding more confident than she felt.

The day of the fair dawned bright and shiny.

The Fab Four were up at 6am, arranging trestle tables (donated by *Pine-U-Like Furniture Co*) and canopies and raffle prizes.

Eclaire, dressed in a magnificent chef's hat made of papier mâché and a blue and white striped apron, covered two whole tables with cakes and sweets. Some parents had made about fifty sandwiches each.

Of course, all the mums and dads had offered to help at the stalls, but Eclaire had told them firmly,

"It's to be run by kids. That's part of the, um, charity thing. You know, kids taking action on behalf of poorer kids." She didn't want too many adults hanging around asking difficult questions about where exactly the money was going.

Lizzy had decided to make the most of her hair for the day and dressed up as Medusa. She had tied forty rubber snakes (borrowed from *Trix or Treetz Joke Shop*) to the ends of her already snake-like mane.

"Great news!" said Owl, who was wearing an old sack and a beret. "Lady Bolmondely-Fossington-Stokes is going to give prizes and make a speech!"

There were groans from little Brian Hayseed, Owl's sister Loretta and Lizzy's brother Ernie, who had at last got his wish to have a Doom Warriors painting stall.

Lady Bolmondely-Fossington-Stokes lived in a mansion at the top of the hill and behaved as though she were the Queen. She was wheeled out for all the local school fairs. Her speeches, famous for their length, had sent more kids to sleep and more parents scurrying off to the pub than even the town mayor's speeches.

"Well, that will end the day with a snore, then," said Eclaire, peering closely at Owl. "Just what are you supposed to be, Owly?" she asked. "Is that a sack?"

"I am Robin Hood," said Owl. "And Brian is Maid Marian, see?"

Little Brian Hayseed blushed under his Maid Marian cap. He liked this costume better than the last one he had worn, which had been when he was playing a tree stump in the school play.

"Oh, well. It takes all sorts," muttered Loretta, who was looking extremely fetching in a gypsy outfit.

Owl had rigged up an impressive tent (loaned for the day by *Marquee-U-Luv*) on which she had pasted the sign: *Freak Show.*

"What!" said Flash, aghast.

"I thought it s-sounded better than 'Cabaret,'" said Owl. "And, you know, we have got Tiger Boy..."

Flash sighed, but there was no time to worry about details now. They still had to build the stage for the Freak Show out of forty orange boxes (donated by Honest Harry from the market) and rig up posts to hitch the ponies to. She'd imagined a

Wild-West-style display, but the stable boy from the riding school had turned up with four of the smallest, quietest ponies and an assortment of hard hats for toddlers. The ponies were little Shetlands – two skewbald, one piebald and one dapple grey. Sweet, but babyish, thought Flash. She had secretly hoped that a polo-playing Prince might turn up and ask her to ride with him, but that hope was fading fast. Still, she would be able to lead four toddlers about on the Shetlands at once...and maybe charge £2.50 each. Heh heh, think of all that dosh. Even so, she had to admit that the ponies looked a bit out of place next to the notice she had painted last night:

By midday, everything was ready. They even had decorations – a hundred balloons (courtesy of *Inflatables-R-Us*) and bunting left over from the Jubilee.

Mrs Pinn gazed proudly out of the window, thinking how professional the fair looked.

"It looks really professional," she said to Mr Pinn, who was sitting in his favourite armchair, staring at the wall.

"Hmmmmmmm," said Mr Pinn.

The woodcraft folk had agreed to stand at the entrance and charge visitors 50p to get into the street. It was all looking good. But the Fab Four were worried.

"What if it rains?" worried Owl, looking up at

the clear, blue sky. She had spotted a small cloud in the distance and she was pretty sure it was sailing their way.

"What if no one comes?" worried Eclaire, thinking that even she couldn't eat four hundred sandwiches, and worrying whether they had got the barrels of lemonade on sale or return.

"What if it rains *and* no one comes?" worried Lizzy, who could suddenly think of no reason on Earth why anyone should come, when they could be home watching TV and picking their noses and arguing like most families.

Only Flash's spirits were high and she was right, as usual – because, if it's a nice sunny Saturday and there's a jumble sale round the corner, people do come. If it's a jumble sale and a Freak Show and pony rides and fortune telling and mystery celebrities, then *lots* of people come.

Sure enough, people were soon pouring in and the woodcraft folk, all of whom had dressed up as small woodland creatures, were run off their paws counting change.

And still more and more people came.

And more and more. There seemed to be far

more people streaming in than had ever been to any of the local school fairs and jumble sales. Lizzy had a sneaky, and not very nice, feeling that she knew the reason why... But she suppressed it and soon started enjoying herself, because everything was going so incredibly well.

The queue for the ponies snaked up and down the street twice!

The sweet and cake stall was a riot. The sight of so many small rabbits and fairies and clowns stuffing themselves with Nuclear Nougat brought a tear to Eclaire's eye.

Ernie's Doom Warriors stall was surrounded by about fifty nerdy twelve year olds. They were all swapping models and holding auctions and queuing to paint the little figures, while Ernie was overcharging outrageously!

The jumble stall was cleared in minutes and Lizzy sold all the raffle tickets in an hour!

Even things that looked like turning into disasters magically seemed to turn out all right. Lizzy thought that it was just as if the fairy godmother she had wished for earlier had chanced to fly overhead and said, "Yes! I see that today is the day of the Fab Four's summer fair, which will save the future happiness of the Pinn family! And so I will sprinkle some fairy dust upon them all to ensure that everything goes spankingly well!"

"I'm making a fortune here," said Loretta, grinning from her fortune teller's tent. Since Astra Turf had not shown up, Loretta, luckily already togged up in gypsy earrings and a spotted headscarf, had boldly filled the gap. She had swiftly billed herself as the great-great-great-great-granddaughter of Gypsy Rose Lee – and everyone had believed her.

She was just telling a handsome young man that he was soon to fall in love with a beautiful, young actress called Loretta, when a small round infant stuck its head in the tent and said, "Oy! You're not a gypsy! You're Loretta Smith! Oy, you're a cheat!"

But, even this incident was saved, as Eclaire

whisked the infant off, bribed him with Nuclear Nougat to keep his mouth shut, and the handsome young man winked at Loretta and said, "See you later, I hope."

Everyone was in a party mood and everyone seemed happy to spend, spend, spend. And both of the local papers had sent photographers!

The reporter from the *Gazette* took Eclaire aside for an interview and told her what a marvellous job she was doing and how she was following in the footsteps of her fabulous father. This all went to Eclaire's head a bit, and she posed for several photos with toddlers and old ladies.

"Let's have a photo of you with a handful of fivers!" said the reporter from the *Gazette*. Eclaire happily obliged.

If the Fab Four had had time to think, they would have thought, This is *fantastic*! This is totally *amazing*! This is just too good to be true! But they didn't have time. They were too busy charging round taking money.

"Your dad is going to be *loaded*!" said Flash,

gleefully.

"Shh!" hissed Eclaire, noticing that the *Gazette* reporter was still taking pictures.

And by 6pm, which was the time for the grande finale of the Freak Show and the speech and prizes, they had sold almost everything that possibly could be sold and quite a lot of things, like Eclaire's mum's cutlery and plates and Lizzy's mum's tablecloth, which shouldn't.

But nothing could dampen their spirits now.

The fairy godmother smiles on us, thought Lizzy. She really does. But the fairy godmother was heading for a fall...

Five

At 6pm, little Brian Hayseed announced the Freak Show, and Fifi and her Performing Fleas took to the stage. Owl was sitting at the front and said later that there definitely *was* a flea on Fifi's arm, but no one else could see anything at all. All they could do was watch as Fifi, dressed in her mum's best curtains (unfortunately, without her mum's permission, but that is another story), pirouetted around the stage, describing the fleas' performances.

"And this is Eric! The most amazin' flea of all!" she warbled, "'E can jump fifty times 'is own height and somersault fifty times on the way down! Watch!"

Everyone watched with baited breath. Flash could swear that she saw everyone's heads go up and down, as Eric did his jump.

"Oh, no," she thought. "They'll be throwing rotten tomatoes in a minute. But they weren't. It seemed as if nothing could spoil the party mood, as Fifi's next invisible flea, Petunia, rode a tiny unicycle up and down Fifi's back.

Everyone cheered like mad as Brian stamped on to introduce "Nia the Nectar-throated Nightingale" because Nia the Nightingale had insisted he added that bit at the last moment. Unfortunately, Brian stuttered a bit, so it came out as "Nia the Nectar-nosed Nightingale", but everyone cheered as if he'd introduced the Queen herself. As it turned out, Nia sounded like "Clara the Concrete-encrusted Crow". But no one in the audience seemed to care. Nia swooped offstage regally, announcing that she'd be performing at Covent Garden in a matter of weeks.

"Singing? Or flower selling?" muttered Flash. But she couldn't help feeling sorry for poor old Vernon the Ventriloquist.

"Didn't anyone tell him that

ventriloquists aren't supposed to move their lips?" whispered Owl. But obviously nobody had, and nobody cared, either.

"Why are they all being so nice?" wondered Lizzy, as Tiger Boy, who had quite obviously made his tiger suit out of a couple of old striped cushions, exited to wild applause.

Fire-eating Freddy, who snuffed out two matches and a small candle with his tongue, and then squealed and had to be hosed down by Bert Drench because a birthday cake candle caught fire in his hair, was generously applauded. Even Magda the Witch, who had to be carted off weeping, because her pet frog hopped offstage before she'd even started saying her spell, was enthusiastically cheered.

"Why is everyone being so kind?" whispered Flash to Eclaire.

"I've got a horrible idea why it might be," whispered Eclaire. "They don't care how bad this all is. They've just come to see Prince Harry and Wills!"

"Oh, no! Of course! We'll *have* to do something to rescue the situation!" hissed Flash. "Thank goodness old Orpheus Clang's on next. He should drone on for long enough..." They sneaked round the back of the stage to find little Harry Hawkins and William Snagg. They were nowhere to be found. "We'll have to use Brian and Ernie..." whispered Flash feverishly.

Orpheus Clang rose up to a smattering of polite applause. Even this audience, generous and eager as it was, could only take so much.

Orpheus wore a dinner jacket, bow tie and very self-satisfied expression. He strolled onstage as though he had all the time in the world. But he hasn't, thought Flash, even this lot won't stand him for long.

As soon as Orpheus started, Flash knew that she was right:

"Oh, lucid, lustrous, shines the star,
above our little town
and we have travelled from very far
and put on our brightest gown.
Because we must a journey make
the bravest and the boldest
and for it we must bake a cake
to feed our youngest and oldest..."

Oh, Lucid, Lustrous, shines the Star

On droned Orpheus, while Owl listened in mounting horror, as he murdered the English language. Flash and Eclaire plotted furiously behind the scenes, forcing makeshift crowns onto the heads of little Brian Hayseed and Ernie.

"We can't do it!" they shouted.

"It's for a good cause!" said Eclaire firmly, sitting on Brian to keep him in one place while she tied a cloak round him. "You'll just *have* to pretend that *Prince Wills and Prince Harry* is the name of your act! Otherwise, we'll all be murdered!"

"We'll be murdered anyway, when they realise

that there aren't any real princes here!" wailed Ernie.

Oh, goodness, thought Eclaire. He's right. There's no way out.

And, sure enough, from the front of the stage, she could hear the crowd growing restless.

Then someone shouted, "OK, Orpheus. Thanks very much, but we want Wills and Harry."

"Oh, erm, but I have here a gorgeous ode to Wills and Harry, which I am just about to read. It is only, er..." Orpheus riffled through a huge handful of sheets, many of which fluttered away in the stiff breeze that had just blown up and were thankfully lost for ever... "It's only, er, 40, erm, 39... 38 pages long..."

"We want Harry! We want Wills!" The shouting grew louder.

The slow handclap started.

Ernie and Brian wriggled free and leapt over the nearest hedge.

Owl rushed to Eclaire and Flash. "What are we going to dooooo?"

But, just at that moment, there was the most

fantastic din, drowning out even the loudest jeering and booing of the crowd. The little cloud that Owl had so gloomily spotted earlier had indeed become a very big cloud – and had brought with it the most stupendous storm. Thunder crashed and rolled like drum and bass, lightning forked and flashed, and the Shetland ponies broke their ropes in terror and charged down the street! One galloped straight onto the stage through Orpheus Clang's legs, or would have, if the lanky poet hadn't squealed, clung onto the poor creature's mane and vanished into the distance astride the tiny pony, scattering his beloved ode all over the road. Rain poured down in sheets onto the smashed and sodden orange crates. One pony stopped to nibble the giant prize carrot cake, the glory of the cake stall, which was donated by Lady Bolmondely-Fossington-Stokes herself. Another pony buried its nose happily in the edible necklaces. The fourth pony made straight for Lady Bolmondely-Fossington-Stokes herself. She was wearing an irresistible hat that looked to the pony very like a buttercup meadow covered in sugar lumps, but was in fact the creation of local artist Damson Stove.

"Oh, it's a disaster," gasped Eclaire, gazing in horror at Lady Bolmondely-Fossington-Stokes, who appeared to have fainted at the sight of her beloved hat disappearing into the jaws of a wild beast.

"Oh, no!" cried Flash, thinking of what they would say at the stables. "We've got to catch the ponies!"

It's a blessing in d-disguise, thought Owl, as she watched everyone running for cover. I'll be able to say that Wills and Harry were flying in when their helicopter was held up by bad weather.

She rushed over to help the vet, who was reviving Lady Bolmondely-Fossington-Stokes with brandy.

"She'll be fine," whispered the vet. "She's not the first old codger I've revived this way." And he hauled the now wailing and moaning dignitary off to his surgery.

"Look!" shouted Lizzy, just as the vet's van sped off through the deluge, unfortunately whipping the wing mirror off the fire engine and causing Bert Drench to roar off in hot pursuit, shouting "Oy! This vehicle is paid for by the tax payers!"

"*Look*!" shouted Lizzy again at the top of her voice.

Everyone looked. The fairy godmother, thought Lizzy, had definitely hung up her wings for the day. A wicked stepmother had taken over, big time. She had obviously unfurled her bat wings in the storm cloud and was now making things even worse, rather than better.

At the end of the street, there were three figures in snow-white karate outfits, with red bandanas round their heads. They were wearing masks! They somersaulted into the street and the few remaining visitors started to applaud what they thought was another act. Then everyone stopped in mid-cheer, realising that it was the dreaded Karate Gang!

"It's Li," said Eclaire. "I'd recognise those trainers anywhere."

Lizzy gasped. Eclaire was right. A pair of blue and silver trainers were clearly visible under the leader's snow-white suit.

"They're going to take the

cash!" yelled Eclaire, frozen to the spot.

Sure enough, before anyone could move muscle, Li and his gang had whipped the big cash box from the clutches of two terrified woodcraft hedgehogs, leapt on the backs of the three remaining ponies and galloped off down the high street.

Flash shouted at the top of her voice, "Pickles! Whoaaaaaa! Whoaaaaaa!" And the dapple gray mare stopped dead in her tracks, catapulting her rider into a hedge.

Flash ran like the wind through the driving rain. She dived at the white figure entangled in the hedge. "Drat!" she gasped. It was no longer someone in a white tunic, but a white tunic all on its own. Somehow, the culprit had wriggled out and vanished.

"Call the police!" shouted Eclaire, but there was no one left to hear.

Only the Fab Four and Loretta were left, drenched, amid a sea of shattered orange boxes. A river was running down the middle of the street, in which floated a few Doom Warriors, a couple of Karamel Kalashnikovs and a necklace made of Brussels sprouts and cherry tomatoes.

I'll never be allowed to work at the riding school

again, thought Flash. And that means I'll never ride again...

I'll never be in another play, thought Owl. When everyone hears how I can't even organise a Freak Show with *one* good act, they'll just laugh at me...

The wicked stepmother has done her worst, thought Lizzy. And my best friend will move south and we will spend weeks paying for all this damage...

I will go to jail... thought Eclaire, as she realised that she had mistakenly sold a set of silver knives and forks for 20p.

The first to speak, as the thunder died down, was Lizzy. "Well, at least we've got all the money from the stalls and rides and everything. They only got the entry money. Let's go and count that."

Eclaire brightened, but one look at Owl told her the truth. Owl's little round face suddenly looked like the face of a long droopy bloodhound.

"Oh, Owly, you didn't!" was all that Eclaire said.

But Owl had. Just before the freak show, she had scuttled round, collecting all the money together and had put it all in the one box.

"It was a p-proper cash b-box, you s-see, with a p-padlock," she mumbled, her tears mingling with the rain. "I th-thought it would be safer..." she trailed off.

There was nothing else to do but trudge home.

But, when Eclaire got home, Mr Pinn was not there.

Mrs Pinn was pretending that everything was all right, but Eclaire could see that it was not.

"What's happened? Where's he gone?" she squeaked.

"I don't know!" said Mrs Pinn and burst into tears. "He got a phone call from the local paper and went out, saying that he had to go away suddenly. He wouldn't tell me where he was going." Mrs Pinn shook her head. "And, it's the first time he's got out of his chair all week!"

Eclaire banged on the wall for Lizzy, who came charging straight round with Flash and Owl. They had all been phoning the police at Lizzy's.

"My Dad's gone missing," said Eclaire, bursting into howling sobs yet again and flinging herself onto Mrs Pinn's thin lap.

Flash felt faint. She suddenly had an extremely

clear memory of the look on her own mum's face when her dad had left. It had been just like the haunted expression on Mrs Pinn's face... "He'll be back," she said, as cheerfully as she could. "He'll be back."

"We'll stay here with you tonight, to comfort you," said Lizzy. "If that's OK with you, Mrs Pinn?"

Eclaire's mother just nodded weakly.

And they all rolled up together, exhausted, in Eclaire's big pink and purple duvet.

Things must start getting better again, thought Lizzy, as she drifted off to sleep. It's the fairy godmother's turn to reappear, surely.

But it wasn't, not yet.

Six

"Claire! Elizabeth! Emily! Harriet! Come down this minute!"

The Fab Four were woken by the hysterical shouts of Mrs Pinn the next morning. They shuffled downstairs wondering what had gone wrong *now*?

Mrs Pinn, looking like an electrocuted telegraph pole, was standing at the foot of the stairs, her eyes blazing.

"What is the meaning of this?" she screamed, in a voice like a demented hyena. And she thrust the local paper at them.

On the front page were two pictures of Eclaire. One picture showed her cuddling two toddlers and an old lady. In the other, she was her grinning and waving fistfuls of fivers. The headline was:

CHARITY CHEATS

Shocking behaviour of local bigwig in festival fiasco

The Fab Four read on:

While local resident 83-year-old Elsie Bogweed lives on a can of dog food a day and tragic three-year-old Tania waits for her life-giving bone-marrow transplant, an able-bodied father-of-three, former councillor Mr Percival Pinn, has embezzled money to keep him in his comfortable home.

"We thought that the street festival was raising money for charity," said Mr Vine, wine merchant. "I had generously donated a case of our best vintage to the dear little girl who came round for the raffle. If we'd known the money was just to line the pockets of the wealthy, we would certainly not have gone to all that trouble."

"It was bad enough getting Gran's wheelchair here, especially to see Prince William – and he didn't even turn up! I don't know why we pay these royals so much," said an enraged mum-of-five. "To find out our own neighbours were ripping off our money too, was dreadful."

"It's an absolute disgrace," added estate agent, Mr Fleecem. "I turned up, hoping for a lovely day out with the kiddies and was treated to a pathetic freak show that looked as though it was slung together by street urchins. And to think that my hard-earned money has just gone straight into these people's pockets. There ought to be a law against it."

Well, there is a law against it – and the Gazette is determined to see that the law breakers are brought to justice!

Neighbours say that the Pinn family didn't want to move to a rough area with little bedrooms. Let's see how they like a prison cell!

The Fab Four gazed aghast. The worst part of the article was the captions:

"Clara Pinn cons the kiddies."

"In the money? You bet, suckers!"

"They haven't even spelt your name right!" spluttered Flash.

But the others were lost for words. The full enormity of what they'd done came crashing down on their heads.

At that ghastly moment, there was the sound of

a key in the lock and Mr Pinn walked in.

"Percy!" cried Mrs Pinn, hurling herself upon him.

"Dad!" cried Eclaire, following suit.

After a minute of weeping, during which the rest of the Fab Four contemplated the carpet and wished that it would swallow them up, Mr Pinn extricated himself from his weeping womenfolk and said drily, "Just as well the boys aren't home. I'd have been suffocated."

"Er, well, we'll be off then," said Lizzy, trying to edge past him to the front door.

"I don't think so," said Mr Pinn. "I think we all need a little talk."

The girls all knew what 'little talk' meant, when said in that tone of voice. It meant that the adult in question would rant and rave and you would wish you were in Siberia, or dead.

But they were defeated. Meekly, they trooped off after the Pinns, who led the way into the front room.

First, Mr Pinn sat down. Then, agonisingly slowly, he read the front-page story.

"Hmmm. As I thought," he said. "I have,

naturally, been to see my boss and warned him of this. Since he has already moved to the south of England," he continued, raising his eyebrows at the still-twitching Mrs Pinn, "I had to get an overnight train. I'm sorry I didn't explain, but I thought I would get back before you heard about it. I was worried about your nerves."

"Oh, that's fine, dear," squealed Mrs Pinn, wriggling like a puppy who's been offered a particularly tasty biscuit. "But can't we go through all this later? You're back, and that's what matters."

"No. I'm afraid we can't. There's no time to lose. As I expected, my boss immediately withdrew the job offer. He said that the company was in bad shape and couldn't afford further scandal. So now, Claire," he turned to Eclaire, who was pink with shame and wet with tears, "things are even worse than before. We'll still have to sell up and move somewhere smaller, but I haven't *got any job at all!*"

Eclaire hiccupped and tried to say sorry, but her father was getting redder and crosser by the second. "Sorry is not good enough! Now,

I must immediately make a cheque out to a real charity to try to clear what remains of the Pinn family name! So, I must know exactly how much money you raised! How much was it? To the nearest penny!"

"We don't know," said Eclaire.

"*YOU DON'T KNOW*!?" bellowed Mr Pinn.

"No. You see, the cash box was s-stolen... but we know whodunnit," whispered Eclaire.

"They've reported it to the police, of course," squealed Mrs Pinn, alarmed at the sight of her husband, who was advancing towards Eclaire with a face like thunder.

Just then, the doorbell rang. When Mrs Pinn opened it, there stood PC Bigfoot, the reins of four very tired-looking ponies in one hand and a cash box in the other.

"These anything to do with you, ma'am?" he said.

"Good heavens, those poor ponies!" exclaimed Mrs Pinn.

Flash immediately dashed out and started hugging and kissing the bedraggled ponies.

"I'll have to take them straight back to the

stables," she shouted, relieved to be making her escape.

"But look, he's got the cash box too!" yelled Eclaire.

PC Bigfoot entered the room. Very slowly and ceremoniously, he placed the cash box on the Pinns' pristine coffee table. Mrs Pinn winced.

"It's filthy," she said.

"We found it behind a bush, madam," said PC Bigfoot. "Unfortunately, the culprits, whom eye-witnesses believe to be the Karate Gang, have not yet been apprehended, at this moment in time."

"At which moment in time are you considering apprehending them?" asked Mr Pinn sarcastically.

Bigfoot sighed and continued reading from his notebook. "The four animals must be signed for, before I can release them from custody. There are claims for damages pending as to the following: one hat, made by Ms Damson Stove, owned by Lady Bolmondely-Fossington-Stokes..."

"Please officer, can't this wait? Let us please first count the cash and try to find the criminals. My daughter says that she knows the name of one of the gang."

"Many people say they know the names of the Karate Gang, madam, but, at this moment in time, none has been found to be correct, as yet," sighed Bigfoot, snapping shut his book, "But you may open the box if you wish to ascertain that all is still within."

Eclaire picked up the box, which was very heavy and still padlocked.

"It's all still there. It weighs a tonne!"

They carried the cash box into the garden, where Mr Pinn, glad to have something to vent his rage on, smashed the padlock with a sledgehammer.

The ponies, who Flash had brought round the side of the house, cheered up immediately at the sight of the garden. They started munching everything in sight, but Mrs Pinn was beyond caring.

The Fab Four, the Pinns and PC Bigfoot watched eagerly as Eclaire lifted the lid. At last, they would know how much they had raised.

The reason the cash box had felt very heavy was that it contained a brick. The brick was wrapped in a note and the note said:

"No one messes with the Karate Gang. And no one messes with Li wei Chang. You have been warned."

Mrs Pinn, whose nerves, never steady at the best of times, had been stretched to breaking point by the events of the last few hours, keeled over in a faint.

"Elaine!" cried Mr Pinn, rushing to her side. PC Bigfoot immediately rolled Mrs Pinn into the recovery position and took her pulse.

Lizzy fled next door for her mum, who had years of experience in dealing with Mrs Pinn's nerves. While Mrs Wigan was reviving her neighbour with lemon tea, Mr Pinn showed her the *Gazette*.

"Lizzy!" said her mum in horror. "You mean that the fair wasn't for charity? But that's terrible!"

"B-but we were t-trying to save Eclaire from

moving, and save Mr Pinn too! " exclaimed Lizzy.

Mr Pinn was unmoved. He dialled the police.

"But the police are, I mean, *is* here!" squealed Eclaire.

"I think we need reinforcements," said Mr Pinn grimly.

"You're not going to have us arrested?"

"I'm going to get Mr Chang arrested. He's the reason I got sacked! And he is the man, obviously, behind the Karate Gang!"

Lizzy's mum took charge, herding Mrs Pinn back into the kitchen and ordering the Fab Four upstairs.

"But you don't understand," said Eclaire. "It isn't Mr Chang! It's his son! He's in our class! And he hates us!"

"Nonsense! This is not the work of a schoolboy! We've had quite enough of your bright ideas for a week. Now, upstairs with the lot of you! And don't come down until you are called!" said Lizzy's mum in her sternest voice.

The four girls moped about in Eclaire's room barely able to speak. Each was wondering how much money had been in the cash box. Even if the Karate

Gang were caught, red-handed, how would the girls ever be able to repay everyone who had come to the fair? What would their schools do? Would they be expelled for lying to the whole neighbourhood? Worse, maybe they would be sent to young offenders' institutions... Flash knew that her mum would get a terrible time of it as a school dinner lady. All the kids would know that her daughter had tried to steal from the poor to give to the rich – and risked ponies' lives into the bargain. Maybe her mum would lose her job!

Eclaire felt worst in some ways and best in others. The good bit was that her father was safe, which suddenly seemed to her more important than anything. The worst bit was that it looked as if she had got her best mates into a very big amount of trouble. "I feel it's all my fault," she said finally. "First, I blab on about moving home, then you all come to my rescue and then I land you in this mess."

"It's not your fault," said Lizzy kindly. "We've *all* been fools."

"Yes," whispered Owl. "I think we sh-should rename ourselves the Foolish Four."

"It'll only be three, anyway," said Eclaire. "We'll be going to an even worse area with even smaller rooms now. I probably won't even *get* a room..."

"Yeah, you'll be in a matchbox with a just a single match to keep you warm," said Flash, in a forlorn attempt to raise everyone's spirits. Then, she spotted the crumpled Karate Gang note, which Eclaire was still clutching. Flash suddenly felt furious.

"Oh, come on!" she said. "You could be in a war zone! Or starving! You know something? We've got to get that money back! Otherwise we'll be jailed for theft. They'll all think we're in league with the Karate Gang, don't you see? They'll think we organised the money to be stolen so that we could split it up between us! And they'll probably blame your dad, as well! We can't just sit here! We've got to do something! We've got to find Li and get the money back!"

"Yesss! We know where he lives. Let's go there now," said Lizzy.

"Um," said Owl.

"Er..." said Eclaire.

"Do we have a chance to make this better? Or are we just going to be wimps?" said Flash. "Who are we? The Feeble Four or the Fab Four?"

And so, before they had any more time to be scared, the Fab Four tiptoed downstairs and crept out of the side door. They heard the wails of Mrs Pinn and the soothing tones of Lizzy's mum echoing from the kitchen, before they fled down the street towards Li's house.

At the corner, Flash stopped suddenly. "How could I have been so thick!" she exclaimed. "We've got evidence!"

The others looked bemused.

"The white tunic! In the hedge!"

As one, the Fab Four raced back through the rain, which looked as though it had been going on all night. And yes, there was the tunic.

"Right," said Flash, grabbing the tunic and stuffing it in her shirt. "Now for Li's house. Owl watches the side entrance. Eclaire keeps an eye on the back. And me and Lizzy do the business."

And, shoulder to shoulder, they set off down the street.

They marched up to Li's door and banged loudly. Flash, brave as she seemed, could feel her heart thudding. Her temples throbbed as though a woodpecker were inside her head, trying to bash his way out. Eclaire's round squashy legs felt as if they were made of frogspawn and her tummy did a somersault with each bang on the door.

"We should have thought this through," she whispered. "Suppose the Karate Gang are lying in wait?"

"Let's go," cried Flash, suddenly panicking.

But at that moment, to their great surprise, Li opened the door in pyjamas and slippers, looking very like a ten-year-old boy with flu, which is what he was.

Flash immediately felt a fool. How could this little boy possibly be in the infamous Karate Gang? But still she said, "Our money or your life."

"Eh?" said Li, rubbing his eyes. Then he spotted Eclaire and tried to slam the door shut. But Lizzy had her foot on the doorstep.

"Mum!" shouted Li.

Mrs Chang appeared and was surprised to see a chef, a cowgirl, a gorgon and a small outlaw in a sack on her front doorstep. The Fab Four had, of course, fallen asleep in their fancy dress of the day before and, in the drama of the morning's events, hadn't got changed. She suppressed a laugh and invited them in, listening carefully to their story from beginning to end. They showed her the note that had been wrapped round the brick.

"I think I know this handwriting!" she exclaimed. "I'm almost sure it's been written by Mr Fleece's secretary! She bombards us with letters because Fleece has been trying to get my husband's company out of town ever since we arrived! He wants to expand his offices! And now he's trying to get our *son* into trouble! How typical of him to get his secretary to do his dirty work!"

"Do you mean Mr Fleecem? But surely *he* can't be behind the Karate Gang? He's an estate agent!"

"Everybody's something or other," said Mrs Chang, with a smile. "And he is exactly the kind of person who would profit from buying up buildings cheaply, which is what someone has been doing to the shops that have been attacked by the Karate Gang."

Lizzy nudged Flash. "She's lying. She's trying to pretect her son," she whispered. "Show her the tunic."

"Well, we think it *was* Li," insisted Flash. "And he was wearing this!" She whipped out the white tunic, managing, Lizzy noticed irritably, to give them all quite a good long view of her brand new bra.

"Maybe the one who left the tunic wasn't Li,"

said Eclaire. "But one of the others was...was... wearing Li's trainers. *And* Li said he was a black belt. So that proves it!"

"Oh, Li!" said his mum, ruffling his hair. "No one's a black belt at ten years old! Not in proper martial arts."

Seeing his embarrassment, she quickly added, "Although he is *very* talented, but at aikido, not karate."

"Well, what about the trainers?" insisted Eclaire, though as she gazed at Li's fluffy, buffalo slippers and remembered the long legs of the Karate Gang, which had dragged in the road as they galloped off on the Shetland ponies, she felt that she was losing her case.

Li finally piped up, "Everyone in school has those trainers. They're a copy of Badidas. They're only a tenner," he added, rather sweetly, Lizzy thought.

"So...er, it wasn't you?" said Eclaire feebly.

"I wouldn't have dared come near you, not after that punch you gave me," said Li, as his mother raised her eyebrows at Eclaire.

"Sorry about that," said Eclaire, blushing furiously. "But you have got an iron stomach."

"Aikido," smiled Li. "Oh, and this." He shyly lifted his pyjama top.

He had a padded bandage all the way round his middle.

"His dad puts it on him to protect him..." said Mrs Chang. "Shall I tell them, Li?"

Li nodded.

"Li had a kidney transplant two years ago. We had to leave our home, and...everyone we loved, to come here...for treatment." Li's mother had a faraway look in her eyes. Eclaire gulped. The Changs had left everything they loved – their whole country! – and she had been kicking up a storm about moving to a new town!

Mrs Chang blinked and smiled. "Of course, my husband has done very well since then, but he lives in fear that Li will be hurt in a fight or something. So, he makes him learn aikido and wear that bandage. Don't worry," she added kindly. "You weren't to know."

"So, um, will you... um, catch Fleecem?" said Lizzy, after one of those silences that seem to last for days.

"I will call the police immediately, but I do think

we need more to go on," said Mrs Chang.

"Wait! The tunic," said Flash. The tunic had two pockets. One of them held two bus tickets and an electricity bill. The bill was addressed to

Josiah Fleecem

Findem, Katchem and Fleecem Ltd.

Estate Agents.

"Now we'll find 'im, catch 'im and fleece *'im*!" chanted the girls, handing the envelope to Mrs Chang.

"Thank you, thank you very much," she said, heading for the phone.

The next week's local paper, the *Bugle*, ran a very different story:

HAVE-A-GO HEROINES TRAP KARATE GANG

The TRUE STORY behind the Street fair of 'Cheats'

Our rival paper, the Gazette, published slander last week about Mr Percival Pinn, local councillor and pillar of the community. But, Mr

Pinn's family and friends are following in his footsteps to create a better neighbourhood for us all! His daughter and her friends have, according to police sources, succeeded in trapping the infamous KARATE GANG. In a dramatic swoop, three suspected members of the gang were arrested, after a tip-off from Clara Pinn, whose charity money was stolen by the gang. All the money was recovered – a magnificent total of £4,062.12!

This money, far from going to line the Pinns' own pockets, will go towards a lifetime's supply of meals-on-wheels for 83-year-old Elsie Bogweed, a life-giving bone-marrow-transplant for three-year-old Tania and to help towards a kidney-transplant programme funded by Artsmart's new proprietor – Mr Chang.

Mr Pinn, meanwhile, is being made manager of Chang's Artsmart, which has donated a year's supply of art supplies to every school in the town. The Bugle looks forward to backing Mr Pinn's campaign for re-election to our council next year and we hope Mr Chang will soon be joining him!

Police Constable Bigfoot said last night, "We are unable, at the present moment in time, to reveal the identities of the Karate Gang, but can tell you that Mr Fleecem, the estate agent, has been taken in for questioning."

You can rely on the Bugle to trumpet the truth!

Seven

"All for one and one for all
Fatty, skinny, short and tall
Frizzy, Flash, Owl and Eclaire
Stick together, foul or fair.

"Four for one and one for four
Funny, clever, rich and poor
Frizzy, Flash, Eclaire and Owl
Stick together, fair or foul."

"I declare this meeting well and truly open! And it is to be a Celebration of the Utter Fabness of the Utterly Fab Four!" said Lizzy happily the next day, as the Fab Four nestled among her hair potions, which seemed to have crept all over the floor again, despite her attempts to beat them back.

"We have raised £4,000 for charity! We have

caught the Karate Gang! We are the best!" chanted Flash and Lizzy.

"But...w-we haven't, really," said Owl.

"I know," said Eclaire. "And I've been thinking..."

"Yes?" said Flash, irritated.

"It wasn't *our* money that was stolen," said Eclaire. "We stole it, don't you see? We got it from everyone under false pretences."

"Oh, that's a bit harsh," said Lizzy. "I mean, everyone had a good time..."

"Only because they th-thought they were going to see royalty. That's the only r-reason they clapped the lousy freak show," said Owl miserably.

"Not true," said Lizzy stoutly. "OK, Owly, so the freak show wasn't your finest hour, but the cakes and sweets and jumble and pony rides and–"

"Yes!" said Eclaire, "but it was all a lie, wasn't it? We said it was for charity!"

"And those poor ponies," said Flash, forlornly. "They could have been run over, or broken their legs!"

"I've been thinking very hard about all this," continued Eclaire. "We did something wrong, but for the right reasons. Then, we did something right, but for the wrong reasons."

"Eh, wh-what?" asked Owl, confused.

"We lied about the charity stuff – that was wrong, but done with good intentions. Then, we ended up helping to catch the Karate Gang, but really we were just trying to s-save our skins!"

"True," said Lizzy. "You know, Eclaire, you're not just a poet and a chef, you're a philosopher, too."

"I suppose I *could* open a cafe with, er, a poem and a thought for the day on the menu..."

"Then your dad would never have to work again!"

"But *you* will, though," said Lizzy's mum, bursting in and waving a big sheet of paper. "You're going to have to clean cars and wash up all through the school holidays to pay this lot off!"

The Fab Four sat back, annoyed. Why was it, they thought, that parents just pushed into kids' rooms, but they always yelled at kids to knock first? They listened reluctantly, and with deepening gloom, as Lizzy's mum reeled off a list of horrors:

"You have to find the money for the following:

"One hat, made by Ms Damson Stove, owned by Lady Bolmondely-Fossington-Stokes.

Wing mirror, fire brigade.

Repairs to tack for riding stables: two missing stirrups, one broken brow band, one pair missing reins, torn girth.

Vet's bills for one pony: chest infection..."

Flash interrupted Lizzy's mum at this point with anxious enquiries about which pony had been treated and would it live, which, apparently, it would.

Lizzy's mum continued:

"Dry cleaning for one pair velvet curtains ruined by Fifi and her performing fleas.

Two woodcraft folk hedgehogs and one squirrel suit (replacement).

Six woodcraft folk badgers and four voles (dry cleaning).

Set of silverware: six knives, six forks, six soup spoons (Mrs Pinn).

Tablecloth (Mrs Smith).

Two trestle tables and leg of further trestle to Pine-U-Like.

Reimbursement of 38 rubber snakes to Trix or Treetz Joke Shop.

Landscaping of two traffic islands and re-turfing of eighteen front gardens trampled by ponies.

Dry cleaning of tailcoat, plus reimbursement for two sessions of aromatherapy for his nerves for Mr Orpheus Clang, poet.

Replacement tent for Marquee-U-Like.

Replacement bunting for Jubilee Fund.

"They were hoping to use it again in twenty-five years time, apparently," Lizzy's mum said with raised eyebrows. "And here's the bill!" she finished, with a flourish.

The bill was enormous.

"Oh no! That stupid hat alone cost £250!" shouted Lizzy.

"Irreplaceable, a work of art, according to Lady Bolmondely-Fossington-Stokes," laughed her mum. "But I'm afraid you're going to have to find a way to pay for it. Here's a snack to cheer you up while you hatch a plan."

"I'll have to move in with you after all, Lizzy," said

Eclaire, as they munched their way through a stack of excellent banana and brown sugar sandwiches. If my mum finds out it was me who sold her silver..."

"But," began Lizzy, then checked herself. There was no need to hurt Eclaire's feelings by admitting that Mrs Wigan had said she couldn't move in.

"Mmmm," she continued. "Although, maybe I'd better move in with you. My mum's best friend works at *Trix or Treetz.* And she lent me those stupid snakes.

"Oh, um," blushed Eclaire, unable to imagine her parents putting up with Lizzy's clutter.

"Oh, stop winding each other up, you two," laughed Flash. "Everything's still great, really. We'll just have to think of a way to raise all that money."

"But how on Earth will we do it?" wailed Eclaire.

"It'll take all summer, that's for sure," said Lizzy.

"Not necessarily," said Owl, smiling shyly. "Let's have a street fair."

"Owly! How *could* you?"

"Only a joke," laughed Owl, as she disappeared beneath a hail of banana and brown sugar sandwiches.

Read more about

Frizzy Lizzy, Flash,
Eclaire and Owl

in the other FAB FOUR books.

The
FAB
Four
Three's
a
Crowd
Ros Asquith

One

"I'm not going. I'm not beginning to go. I'm not starting to begin to go. I'm not even going to *think* about going any more." Such was Owl's resolution as she stared, glummer than glum, at the yellow leaflet for *Kamp Krazy Kingdom – Where Adventure Never Ends.*

"Never ends. Huh. Never begins. Not for me. NO WAY," grumbled Owl. She scanned the brochure for signs of hope. It was packed with 'fun' activities. Hooray! White-water canoeing! Abseiling! Archery! Pole vaulting! Right up Owl's street. Not.

Yum, yum, thought Owl. I can imagine one or two things I'd rather do. Like octopus wrestling. Or perhaps sitting at the bottom of a very deep well for a week...

And the camp was on an island! Across water – virtually abroad!

I'm not even going to mention this trip to mum, Owl thought. She need never even know about it. I'll just tell the teachers that I can't go.

Relieved at this brainwave, Owl scrunched up the leaflet. Unfortunately, in Owl's bedroom, which was the size of a mouse's shoe box, or would have been, if mice had shoes, there was no waste paper bin. She glanced round, which didn't take long. Tiny bunk bed above teeny weeny desk. Postage-stamp wall covered in theatre posters. Toddler-size beanbag. Goldfish bowl. But, strong as Owl's desire to avoid her school trip was, she was not about to risk poisoning her goldfish with shredded leaflet. So, she chucked it out of the window (the leaflet, not the goldfish).

Immediately, a furious voice screeched "Litterbug!"

Typical. This was her mother's one day of the century for tidying up the garden.

"What's this? Oh. Em! Brilliant! You've got a school trip! Why didn't you tell me?"

Owl thought fast.

"N-no, it's nothing. Just something I p-picked up... at the l-library."

"Oh. Well, don't go throwing rubbish about."

Phew.

But Owl's deception lasted just three days.

On the fourth day, she returned from school to find her mother waving an official looking letter addressed to "The parent or guardian of Emily Smith..."

"Em," said her mother in her kindest voice. "The school is asking why we haven't returned the school trip forms. That Adventure Club? Remember? The one that you pretended was nothing to do with you?"

"Oh," sighed Owl.

"So, I've sent it back, with the deposit..."

"No! H-how c-could you?" cried Owl as her heart sank.

"Because everyone else will be going and it sounds lovely and I think you'll have a great time."

Owl shook her head. "No. I c-can't go. I h-hate school. I hate school t-trips. None of my friends will be there. ALL my friends are at another, n-nicer school."

Owl was thinking of her three best pals, Lizzy, Claire and 'Flash' Harriet, who, with Owl, made up the Fab Four.

"Em," said her mother kindly, "I think we need a little talk."

So, Em and her mother had a little talk. It was one of those little talks where the mother speaks a lot and the offspring gazes gloomily into the distance, wondering why they were ever born.

Mrs Smith was, naturally, trying her best to be kind. She had worried about Em since she was a small baby, and now that she was older (although still very small), Mrs Smith was still worrying.

Long ago, when little Em had held onto her legs like a limpet, whenever she tried to leave her – even at birthday parties with big chocolate cakes –

all the other mothers had said, "Oh, they're all like that to begin with. Don't you worry, she'll grow out of it." It had been the same at playgroup, nursery, primary school... But, while other shy children had grown out of it, Em never had.

Em's glamorous sister, Loretta, was a livewire, always busy, masses of friends, talented, beautiful, but Em was just... well, quieter than a mouse. Quieter than an ant, really, thought Mrs Smith – after all, mice do a bit of scuffling about and squeaking. Of course, Emily was very brainy, but her mum felt that it was time to take a stand. The shyness had to stop.

"Brains aren't everything, Em. You've got to be a bit more adventurous and get a bit of a social life. They do all these wonderful activities: white-water canoeing, abseiling...! You'll feel so silly if you're the only one who doesn't go. Loretta LOVED her school trips."

Em finally spoke. "I'm n-not Loretta. I do n-not like big groups of people. I do not like g-games and white-water canoeing. I *have* got a social life. I've got the Fab Four. And if you'd sent me to the same school as them, I might have been a happy p-person!"

And with that, she stomped upstairs and wept into the goldfish bowl. (Which wasn't a very good idea, as she then had to spend half an hour cleaning it out in the sudden fear that salt water might change the goldfish into a shark).

Mrs Smith sighed.

When he got home, Mr Smith sighed.

When she got home, big sister Loretta sighed.

"It's all my fault," said Mrs Smith. "I should have made her go out and about more when she was little – I mean, younger."

"Oh, shush," said sensible Mr Smith sensibly. "She'll come out of her shell in her own good time."

"Look, I'll ring Claire. She'll cheer Em up," volunteered Loretta.

Sure enough, bouncy, kind Claire (Eclaire to her closest mates) came bouncing straight round and lolloped upstairs to bang on Em's door.

But Em wouldn't open up.

"Owl. Owly!" cooed Eclaire.

"Go away. I'm d-drowning myself."

"What? In the goldfish bowl?"

"Yes. I'm small enough."

"I've got some Nuclear Nougat." Nuclear Nougat was Em's favourite out of the many amazing sweets Eclaire made.

"I know I'm small, but I'm not f-five years old," sighed Em. "You think Nuclear Nougat can compensate me for the agonies of my soul?"

"Oh, Owl, don't be daft. It's only a stupid school trip."

"They t-told you? You mean you came round here just because you knew that I d-didn't want to go on the school trip?" And Em burst into more tears.

Standing on the other side of the door, Eclaire felt worried. Owl was shy, sure, but not a cry baby. She decided tough talk might work.

"I've called a meeting of the Fab Four!" Eclaire yelled. "My place, tomorrow, at six. Be there or be a wimp. Byeeeee."

Owl felt thoroughly ashamed of herself. She hadn't opened her door to dear old bouncy Eclaire. She had shouted at her dear old worried mum. And she might have poisoned dear old Goldy, who was, after all, a freshwater fish. She *was* a wimp. She spent the next half hour changing the furniture in the goldfish bowl. Goldy could now choose from a cheerful skull, a decorative, ruined castle and a pirate's cannon. She wondered, from time to time, whether he really cared about these things, but she felt he should have some variety.

Then she spent ten minutes blowing her nose and making resolutions. Of course, she decided that she would go to the school trip. It wasn't walking through flames, after all. In fact, it felt much worse than that to Owl. But she told herself that it would be OK and bounced down to tea with a wide smile.

"Sorry about that," she grimaced. "Of c-course I'll go. I'm sure I'll just *love* it to pieces, just l-like

Loretta." She threw her big sister what she hoped was a withering look.

"Are you all right Em? You look very cheerful. You're not running a fever are you?" asked her mum.

"Some people are never satisfied," huffed Mr Smith.

Owl kept up her pretence at breakfast next morning and went into school with a smile so broad it hurt her jaw. Several people asked if she was all right.

"Just fine," she retorted, in an unusually loud voice (almost as loud as a butterfly sneezing), and breezed into class. Everyone was crowded round a noticeboard headlined *Kamp Krazy Kingdom – Where Adventure Never Ends.*

Pinned on it were brochures and lists. Owl's heart skipped a beat. The lists were of cabins they had been allocated. Four in some, six in others.

"Please, please let me be in a cabin with Mrs Ironglove and no one else," whispered Owl to herself.

Mrs Ironglove was the drama teacher who, despite having a voice like a crocodile with laryngitis and the mannerisms of a gorgon, was the only person in the school that Owl felt understood her.

"Oh, please let it be Ironglove." Owl clenched her teeth and approached the noticeboard.

But the first words she heard were: "Oh, baloney, look who we've ended up with."

"Ugh. Emily *Smith*!"

"Shhhhhh! Look who's here!" Three girls called Bernice, Sylvie and Mathadi, kicked each other and turned round to peer at Owl, who walked calmly by, biting her lip, pretending she hadn't heard a word.

Bernice and Sylvie giggled, but Mathadi came up to Owl later and said, "Sorry about that. They didn't mean nothing by it."

"I don't know what you're talking about," mumbled Owl, blushing.

"Suit yourself," said Mathadi, running off.

Great, thought Owl. Someone tried to be nice to me – and I blew it. I've ended up with big bully, bossy-boots Bernice, smirking, soppy, stupid Sylvie and meek, mild, mealy-mouthed Mathadi, who won't want to speak to me ever again. I have got the worst, the very, very worst group of girls I could possibly have had in the whole world. I have to find a way to escape.

Frock Shock!

Eclaire's happy being fat, but her pencil-thin mum has got other ideas. Can Eclaire escape the horrors of the Twigs and Jumbos club and keep fat rather than fit?

Bad Hair Day

Frizzy Lizzy has tried everything ever invented to tame her wild hair. Can her brother's chemistry set succeed where all else has failed? When you're as desperate as Lizzy, anything's worth a go...

The Love Bug

Flash normally prefers mucking out to making out, but when she meets the gorge new stable lad, Tom, her favourite pony, Flame, is quickly forgotten. Will Flash come to her senses in time to save Flame from the knacker's yard? And who's going to give Flash some top tips on her make-up bag?

Drama Queen

Owl's so shy she's never taken part in anything involving more than two people – even a conversation. But Owl's got big dreams and nothing's going to stop her being in the school play. Will she get the starring role or should she play something a little quieter, a piece of scenery perhaps?

More Orchard Red Apples

Title	Author	ISBN	Price
☐ **Bad Hair Day**	Ros Asquith	1 84121 480 9	**£3.99**
☐ **Frock Shock**	Ros Asquith	1 84121 482 5	**£3.99**
☐ **The Love Bug**	Ros Asquith	1 84121 478 7	**£3.99**
☐ **Drama Queen**	Ros Asquith	1 84121 476 0	**£3.99**
☐ **All for One**	Ros Asquith	1 84121 362 4	**£3.99**
☐ **Three's a Crowd**	Ros Asquith	1 84121 360 8	**£3.99**
☐ **Pink Knickers Aren't Cool**	Jean Ure	1 84121 835 9	**£3.99**
☐ **Girls Stick Together**	Jean Ure	1 84121 839 1	**£3.99**
☐ **Girls Are Groovy**	Jean Ure	1 84121 843 x	**£3.99**
☐ **Boys Are OK!**	Jean Ure	1 84121 847 2	**£3.99**
☐ **Do Not Read This Book**	Pat Moon	1 84121 435 3	**£4.99**

Orchard Red Apples are available from all good bookshops,
or can be ordered direct from the publisher:
Orchard Books, PO BOX 29, Douglas IM99 1BQ
Credit card orders please telephone 01624 836000 or fax 01624 837033
or visit our Internet site: www.wattspub.co.uk
or e-mail: bookshop@enterprise.net for details.

To order please quote title, author and ISBN
and your full name and address.
Cheques and postal orders should be made payable to 'Bookpost plc.'
Postage and packing is FREE within the UK
(overseas customers should add £1.00 per book).
Prices and availability are subject to change.

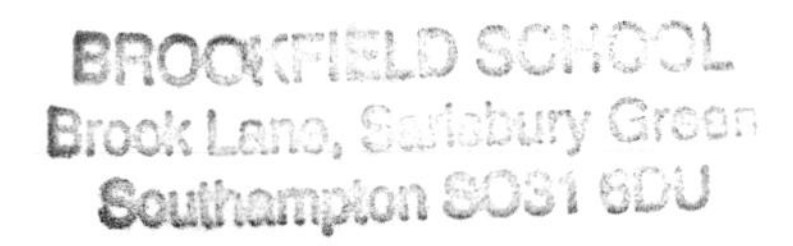